OLD MACDONALD HEARD A PARP

For Tuesday and Cissy

First published in paperback in Great Britain by HarperCollins *Children's Books* in 2017

1 3 5 7 9 10 8 6 4 2

ISBN: 978-0-00-824148-3

HarperCollins *Children's Books* is a division of HarperCollins *Publishers* Ltd.

Text and illustrations copyright © Olaf Falafel 2017

Visit our website at www.harpercollins.co.uk

Printed and bound in Spain

OLD MACDONALD HEARD A PARP

Olaf Falafel

HarperCollins *Children's Books*

Old MacDonald heard a parp...
E-I-E-I-O!

He thought that parp came from a cow ...
E-I-E-I-O!

He thought that parp came from a duck...
E - I - E - I - O!

Old MacDonald heard a parp...
E-I-E-I-O!

He thought that parp came from a goat ...
E-I-E-I-O!

Old MacDonald heard a parp...

He thought that parp came from a unicorn ...

But that was just a dream.

Old MacDonald heard a parp...
E-I-E-I-O!

He thought that parp came from a pig...
E-I-E-I-O!

Old MacDonald heard a parp...
E-I-E-I-O!

He thought that parp came from a horse...
E-I-E-I-O!

Turns out that parp came from ...